POINT HOPE
INSTINCTS

Instincts Point Hope a work of fiction. References to real people, events, establishments, organizations, or locales are intended only to provide the sense of authenticity and are use fictitiously. All other characters, all incidents, dialogue are drawn from the author's imagination and are not to be seen as real.

Copyright © 2020, 2021. All rights reserved.

Published by Dark Titan Publishing. A division of Dark Titan Entertainment.

Also available in eBook.

Dark Titan Noir is a branch of Dark Titan Entertainment.

Paperback ISBN: 979-8-9856344-6-4
eBook ISBN: 979-8-9856344-7-1

darktitanentertainment.com

WORKS BY TY'RON W. C. ROBINSON II

BOOKS/SHORT STORIES

DARK TITAN UNIVERSE SAGA

MAIN SERIES
Dark Titan Knights
The Resistance Protocol
Tales of the Scattered
Tales of the Numinous
Day of Octagon
Crossbreed
Heaven's Called
The Oranos Imperative
Underworld

COLLECTIONS
Dark Titan Omnibus: Volume 1
Dark Titan Omnibus: Volume 2
Dark Titan Omnibus: Volume 3
Dark Titan One-Shot Collection
Dark Titan One-Shot Collection II
Dark Titan Universe Saga Spin-offs Omnibus: Volume 1

SPIN-OFFS
In A Glass of Dawn: The Casebook of Travis Vail
Maveth: Bloodsport
The Curse of The Mutant-Thing
Trail of Vengeance
War of The Thunder Gods

ONE-SHOTS
Maveth, The Death-Bringer
Mystery of The Mutant-Thing
Shade & Switchblade
Retribution of Cain
The Mythologists
Ambush Bot
Kang-Zhu
Cheeseburger Man
Tessa Balthazar
Elite 5

THE HAUNTED CITY SAGA
The Legendary Warslinger: The Haunted City I
Battle of Astolat: A Haunted City Prequel (KOBO Exclusive)
Redemption of the Lost: The Haunted City II
Helper's Hand: A Haunted City One-Shot

SYMBOLUM VENATORES
Symbolum Venatores: The Gabriel Kane Collection
Hod: A Symbolum Venatores Book
Symbolum Venatores: War of The Two Kingdoms Symbolum Venatores: Elrad's Chronicles

EVERWAR UNIVERSE
EverWar Universe: Knights & Lords

PRODIGIOUS WORLDS
Mark Porter of Argoron
Raiders of Vanok
Praxus of Lithonia

FRIGHTENED! SERIES
Frightened!: The Beginning

INSTINCTS SERIES
Lost in Shadows: Remastered
Instincts Point Hope

DARK TITAN'S THE DEAD DAYS
Accounts of The Dead Days

THE HORDE TRILOGY
The Horde
The Dreaded Ones

OTHER BOOKS
The Book of The Elect
The Extended Age Omnibus
The Eleventh Hour: A Chevah Mythos Story
The Supreme Pursuer: Darkness of the Hunt
Massacre in the Dusk
Venture into Horror: Tales of the Supernatural
The Universe of Realms Omnibus: Book 1
The Universe of Realms Omnibus: Book 2
Dark Titan Universe Coloring Book
Dark Titan: Universe of Realms Puzzle Book

THE DARK TITAN AUDIO EXPERIENCE PODCAST
Season 1: Introductions
Season 2: In a Glass of Dawn
Season 2.5: Accounts of The Dead Days
Season 3: Battle For Astolat
Season 4: Hallow Sword: Cursed

POINT HOPE
INSTINCTS

TY'RON W. C. ROBINSON II

THE PLEASURED KILLING

An array of marshals and police officers walk throughout the office building. Many spoke with each other. Others were in the boardroom with detectives discussing cases which culminate between Point Hope and New Haven, Connecticut. In the distance, a desk covered with files containing information on fugitives, murderers, and con artists. The phone rang, the fellow detective at the desk answered.

"This is Brant Harper. United States marshal and detective agent speaking."

Brant is a young detective. Somewhat early in the field. Sitting quietly, listening to the other individual on the phone.

"Yes ma'am. I'll look into that right away. Thank you."

He hung up the phone and looked around the office area. Few detectives and marshals pass by in the office. Brant stood up from his desk, walking toward the filing room. He entered the filing room and went into the system of files. No one else was in the room as he entered. Searching and looking through the file system labeled "*Codenames*" While searching through the files, he stopped upon one, taking the information and printing it out. He approached the printer, waiting for the papers to release. The papers were printed and Brant exited the room. Brant returned to his desk and begun reading the files. He noticed the codename listed above. "*Codename: The Pleasure Man*".

"The Pleasure Man?"

He continued reading the file before stacking it, placing it inside a manila folder and putting it in his desk drawer. He looked at his watch, packed his gear, and left his desk. Brant walked through the area until he was stopped by a fellow detective.

"Sorry to bother you before leaving, Harper. From what I understand, you weren't involved in the warehouse incident that occurred over in New Haven a week ago?"

"No I wasn't." Brant said. "Heard about the incident. Crime bosses meeting in secret. Discussing plots to shake down New Haven. The warehouse being attacked by a vigilante congregation lead by Hoyt Bennett. Last I heard of anything, the agency took care of it."

"Sure they did. The *Instinct* Marshal was one of the leading officials there along with Emily Weston."

Brant looked at his watch again before facing the detective. Time is moving.

"Why are you telling me this?"

"The Chief informed me to tell you you're needed over in New Haven in about another two weeks."

Brant shook his head in disagreement.

"What do you mean I'm needed over there? I have duties to take care of here."

"The Chief's aware of that. Which is why he placed your time slot to the next two weeks. He knows you're currently on a case here."

The Detective walked off as Brant turned his head toward him and back.

"Take care, Harper."

"Same to you."

Brant walked and exited the agency building.

In an undisclosed location elsewhere, a pair of mannequins

sitting on a shelf, covered in blood that appeared to have been smeared upon them by a human hand. The sound of laughter echoes from behind. A man walked into the room, rubbing his hands together. Blood rested on his hands. Wet and warm.

"Only time will tell if they'll ever enjoy the pleasure of my wonderful work."

Brant drove down a street. Passing by homes as leaves fly off the ground as the car passed by. Brant reached over to the passenger seat, pulling up a map. He gazed at the map while driving. Glancing down the areas marked in red ink. The marks indicated locations of which the Pleasure Man was once located. The research was done due to left-behind messages and victims he murdered.

"He's been around."

Inside his home office, Brant sat at his desk, studying the map trying to decipher the Pleasure Man's next possible location. He rubbed his head as he continued staring at the map.

"Only if I could find your next move without you even noticing me. Would it go as planned."

Brant pulled some folders from the drawer. Placing them on the desk next to the map. He searched through the folders, revealing files. The files contain other information on the victims and the locations where they were killed.

He glanced over at the map and to the files and realized that the map was a definitive tool in searching for the Pleasure Man. Brant picks up the phone and contacts his Chief.

"Chief, yes, its Brant. I have discovered some information on the Pleasure Man and I would like to search these locations. If its fine with you."

A slight pause as Brant listened to the Chief.

"Thank you, Chief. I'll get to it immediately."

Brant puts the phone down as the Chief hanged up on the other line. Brant stared at the map and the files.

"If I find these spots, I'll find the Pleasure Man."

The following day, Brant entered through the door of an abandoned home. The home was one of the dotted locations on the map of where the Pleasure Man has once been spotted or sometimes located directly. The electricity of the home was shut off. Brant pulled out a flashlight to search the home, spotting for anything that could be a signal of the Pleasure Man.

Brant walked into the living room of the home. Holding the flashlight in his left hand while his right hand is holding the map and near his weapon on his side. He sees the living room completely cleaned out. No furniture, no home equipment. Just the walls and the floor.

"There has to be something here that could lead to him."

He continued searching, heading into the kitchen. Entering the kitchen, Brant saw the stove, a counter, drawers, but no table for anything to sit on. Not even a dining room table.

"I should check the upstairs area."

He left the kitchen, turning toward the staircase.

He walked up the stairs, seeing three doors. One in front of him, another to his right, and the last one down a hallway near a bathroom. He enters the room in front of him.

Upon opening the door, he saw the room is completely spotless with nothing inside. However, he did notice the room was very clean as if someone was previously inside the home.

"Someone cleaned up well."

Brant left the room and went into the second room, which was to his right.

He opened the door slightly and saw the room was filled with a wooden table and some old furniture. The room appeared to be a storage room. Brant searched the room and was unable to find anything.

He exited, staring down the hall toward the last room. Walking down the hall to the door, he caught the sound of a slight creak from the bottom floor. He decided to take a look back and didn't see anything. He focused his attention back toward the last room. Taking a small glance in the nearby bathroom. Nothing was there to indicate evidence. He opened the last room's door and Brant saw the room was set up as if someone was living there. There was a bed, clothes racked in the closet, and even a flat-screen TV rested on the wall. He scratched his head before walking to the closet. Moving the clothes in the closet and searched them. Finding nothing but old receipts and tissue paper. He searched the drawer, finding nothing but old newspapers and magazines.

"Appears this place isn't the spot."

Brant left the house.

The next location Brant arrived to was an old theater in Point Hope. Seeing no one around as he approached the doors. He enters the old abandoned theater and looks at the map. The theater is placed as the number two location to where the Pleasure Man was last seen.

"Hopefully I can find something here. This looks like his kind of place."

Brant entered, searching the theater in every spot possible. He then opened the double-door room and revealed it was an auditorium with a stage. Used for plays. He walked down the long aisle of the auditorium. Seeing only empty seats and hearing nothing but his footsteps, he approached the stage and walk up the stairs. He took a look at the seats and thought in his mind of how many people would be sitting in those seats while watching a play or a musical. He approached the back rooms. The rooms where the actors and crew would be preparing themselves for their roles in the musicals or plays.

Brant noticed the room was recently used. He's unsure of the reason due to the theater being closed. He did notice the costumes in the closets and the amount of make-up tools that were sitting on the tables along with wigs and hairbrushes and combs. Brant looked at his watch.

"Almost time to return to the office. I'll take one last look."

Brant came up to another room nearby, opening the doors. The room was pitch black with only the light from the sun coming in from the other room. Brant took out his flashlight and saw a pair of mannequins atop a table. The mannequins' faces have been decorated with sinister and creepy smiles, frowns, anger, confusion. Brant pulled out his gun, aiming it toward the mannequins.

"The hell is this?" Brant questioned.

He approached the table, seeing the red coloring on the mannequins. He shined the flashlight on the mannequins, all have been decorated with a red substance. Brant pulled out a cloth, wiping some of the red material and put it in a plastic bag. Brant caught a strange smell, which came from within the room. Tracing the odor, he realized the smell came from the mannequins themselves, particularly the red substance. Brant recognized such a stench.

"Blood."

Shining the flashlight on the rest of the mannequins and seeing that they're all covered with the blood and looked at the one with the smiling face, seeing it has a handprint on the chest made from the blood itself. He spotted a note on the table in front of the smiling mannequin.

The letter said, "*Without pleasure, there can be no true satisfaction.*" Signed, The Pleasure Man. Brant took the letter and threw it onto the table, resting in a small puddle of blood.

"I have to find him."

Brant left out of the auditorium after seeing the blood-covered mannequins. Outside, he approached his car as his cell phone rang. He looked at the ID, seeing it's the office.

"Harper." Brant said.

"We have some major news for you, Marshal."

"Does it relate to the Pleasure Man case?"

"A family of five are being held hostage in their home."

Brant stood next to his car as he listened. He unlocked his car, opening the door. He entered into the car while listening to the office over the phone.

"Where is their home located?"

"In the suburbs. Not far from where you are."

"I'll get there as soon as I can."

An electrical cracking sound came through the phone, interrupting on both ends. Brant looks at the screen, seeing it begin to warp and twist. A glitch? He continued to hear the official on the other side, cracking up.

"I can't hear you clearly through this disturbance. Hello?"

"Is this the marshal that is currently tracking my whereabouts?" Another voice said through the cracking.

"Who is this?" Brant asked. "Who's hacking through this line?"

"By now you should know full well who I am. I'm the guy you're looking for."

Brant paused.

"You're him. The Pleasure Man."

"It's about time we spoke."

"How'd you get this line?"

"I wouldn't concern myself with such pettiness. You're speaking to me, aren't you?"

"Where are you?"

"I'm currently sitting in a suburban home with a family of, about five. Two adults and three children. That's about right."

"I hope you're ready for the two of us to meet in person because I'm on my way there now."

"While, your on your way over here, let's see how fast you can get here to save this family in despair. I feel like teaching them some pleasurable techniques."

"Don't you dare place your hands on that family. If I see a scratch or a slight bruise, I will not hesitate."

"I'm counting on it, Marshal. I'll see you very soon. Don't be late."

Brant heard the screeching screams and hollers in the background.

"You better not harm them! You hear me!"

The phone clicked off with complete silence.

"Damn it!"

Brant started the car, driving at quick speed. Brant speeds down the road, heading towards the suburb home where the Pleasure Man is holding a family hostage. Passing by other vehicles and driving pass stop signs and red lights, nearby causing collisions between cars. He continued to speed up, until he saw a series of suburb homes ahead. Brant took out his phone, pressed speed dial to contact the office.

"Someone pick up." Brant clamored.

Within the office, the ringing echoes as many detectives move continuously through the office. At one desk, an officer picked up the phone.

"Yes."

"I need to speak with the Chief, please. This is Marshal Brant

Harper. On pursuit of the Pleasure Man's location."

"The Pleasure Man?" The officer said. "Right away."

The office gets up from his chair and runs toward the Chief's office. The officer knocks as the Chief looks up.

"What can I help you with?" The Chief asked.

"Brant's on the pursuit of the Pleasure Man as we speak. Do you want me to call in the officials for follow?

"Wait till Brant calls back for details."

"Why?"

"Just do what I say. Brant knows how to operate in these matters."

"Are you sure, sir?"

"He's fine."

Brant drove down the road of the suburban area. Scouting the homes for the exact one, he took small glances at a map and back toward the homes. Seeing no sign, impatience brewed within him. Up to that point, he saw a man standing outside of one home waving in the air. Brant knew such a sight.

"This must be the place."

He pulled up his car and stormed out of it. Running toward the front door. He rammed through the front door, seeing a family. Husband, wife, two sons, and a daughter sitting in the living room. Their hands tied behind their back with duct tape placed on their mouths.

"I'm here to help you."

Brant moved over to them, only to be stopped by the sound of the click of a gun behind him. He froze, slowly turning around to see the Pleasure Man standing in front of him with a gun. The Pleasure Man wore a white mask. No emotion. No life present. Giving himself the appearance of a doll or a walking mannequin.

"It's about time we've come face to face. Now, remove your weapon from your side and slide it over to me."

Brant pulled out his gun from his side slowly, leaning slowly toward the floor. He slid the gun across the living room floor. The Pleasure Man picked it up and set it on the counter. Brant stood still with his hands in the air.

"Isn't this a sight to see. A marshal holding his hands up in the air in the presence of a fugitive."

"I only ask that you do not hurt the family. That's all I-"

"I believe that's the usual cliché we've always heard someone say. Wouldn't you agree, young man?"

The young boy's voice muffled in fear. The Pleasure Man nodded.

"I thought so too."

"This is only between us now." said Brant. "Not the innocent family that's sitting in their own living room tied down and taped."

"The only reason they're here is because I needed a suburb home to use and I love an audience. It gives me great pleasure."

"What would you want? Pleasure or satisfaction?"

"I prefer both." he Pleasure Man chuckled. "The more, the better."

Brant slowly reaches behind his back and pulls out another gun and aims it toward the Pleasure Man.

"Oh!" The Pleasure Man jumped. "Another weapon."

"I will ask you again. Let the family go and it will be settled between you and I."

The Pleasure Man nodded slightly, snatching Brant's other gun from the counter. Holding it up.

"I have a different agenda, Marshal."

He slid the gun back toward Brant, who slowly reached down to pick it up, watching the Pleasure Man stand still. Brant now had both his firearms and only one aimed at the Pleasure Man.

"Looks to me that you've lost this one."

"The show isn't over just yet."

The Pleasure Man reached behind his back, revealing a kitchen knife. He knelt down toward the young boy. The parents attempted to scream, they moved the bodies like tremors, but the duct tape held in their voices. Brant held his gun tightly, aiming at the Pleasure Man.

"Leave the kid alone!"

The Pleasure Man slowly slid the knife across the young boy's throat. Laughing at the scenery.

"You've seen my mannequins. The work I displaced upon them. I believe that

I will need a younger one's blood to complete my next one."

The Pleasure Man pulled back the knife, inching closer toward the boy's throat. The family trembled in horror as Brant fired a shot through the head of the Pleasure Man. He fell to the ground with blood pouring from his head.

Sometime later, the other officials arrived at the scene. Brant walked out of the home, approaching his car. The Chief came over toward him.

"How did it go in there?"

"It went into a necessary cause for action."

The Chief nodded.

"I knew you could handle matters like this."

Brant entered his car.

"So, where's the Pleasure Man?" The Chief asked.

Brant's car backed up into the street as a coroner van pulled up in the driveway. The Chief's face went still.

"Never mind."

The Chief entered the home with other officers at the scene. The coroners came out of the van, taking out the stretcher and the body bag. Brant drove down the street. He glanced at his mirror, seeing the home from behind. He focused his attention back to the road. Ending his mission of the Pleasure Man.

INSTINCTS POINT HOPE

1

Two months after the case of the Pleasure Man was solved, Brant Harper continued his work into other cases which many of his colleagues deemed peculiar to solve. The town is aware of Harper's contributions to them ever since he's been out solving cases and finding more evidence toward unseen killers. The town deemed him a hero. Suggesting he settle on the common cases within the boundaries of Point Hope, Connecticut. Harper often ignored his colleagues regarding the choice of cases and always wanted the ones the others deemed out of the ordinary.

On a foggy day in Point Hope as it occasional is on a clear day, before entering the file office, Detective Smith approached Harper with caution. His hands up near his shoulders with a smirk across his face. Harper stared with a shrug.

"Finally found you." Smith said with a smile. "Others said you would be heading into that room. Even though you're not supposed to go in there."

"What did the Chief tell you to say to me?" Brant questioned. "Did he tell you to watch me if I go ahead and enter the room?"

"Nothing. Other than to stay out of those case files. You know he said they're off limits."

"Off limits? Then, if that was true, the Pleasure Man would not exist and he wouldn't have murdered those people."

"I know you're doing this for the good of the town. Between you and I, this place is already filled with a negative energy. Unlike New Haven, this town is where nightmares are real."

"Nightmares." Brant said with an exhale. "Every place has its round of murderers. It's commonplace."

"I'm not talking about average serial killers or drug lords. There's something different here. Some otherworldly."

"You're thinking of becoming a paranormal investigator or something?"

"No. I know when something's off. As do you."

Harper collected Smith's words before placing his hand on the doorknob. Smith sighed. Harper stood and waited to see what Smith's next motive would be. Would he attempt to stop him from entering the room? Would he let him pass and enter? Or? Would he tell the Chief of Harper's disobedience to the rules? Harper waited and Smith gave him a nod before taking three steps back.

"Good choice." Harper replied.

Searching through the case files, Harper paused on one in particular. Titled, "*The Head-Collector*", Harper grabbed the file and left he office to see Smith standing at the exit, somewhat waiting for him.

"Did you tell the Chief?"

"No. figured you know what you're doing. No reason for me to report this to the Chief."

Harper smirked with relief as he held the file. Smith's eyes turned toward it as Harper waved it. In one glance, Smith caught the tab of the file and read the title. Smith's head went back as he laughed.

"You're not seriously taking on that one are you?"

"It'll be no different than the Pleasure Man."

"I think it will be. Haven't you heard of this Head-Collector?"

"Figure I will once I read what's in this file."

"One thing from me. He's not like the Pleasure Man or any of the average thugs we encountered out in the field. This guy, he's something else."

"He's just a man and this is just a case. Waiting on someone with bravery to solve it."

"You're sure about that?"

"I am." Brant said with confidence.

Brant went and double-checked to see if there were any more files pertaining to the Head-Collector's murders. His purpose for searching is known amongst the officers as there have been multiple files found on certain suspects. As if someone wanted them scattered throughout the office building. Seeing as there weren't any other files on the Head-Collector, Brant left the station to head home.

Once he was home, Harper opened the folder and read everything there was on the Head-Collector. A mysterious individual. A serial killer who decapitates his victims and keeps their heads as his trophies. The history of the Head-Collector intrigued Harper. So much so to the point of uncovering the killings in decades past. Point Hope had always been the residing place for the Head-Collector and somehow he was never caught by the authorities. The same was said of the Pleasure Man, yet, Brant had proved him wrong upon his discovery.

"Alright. Now where do I begin."

Within the file were case photos from the crime scenes. Photos of evidence of potential weapons used in the killings. Photos of the victims. All decapitated and left on the ground either outside or within a building. The records within the file had detailed a number of officers have tried to stop the Head-Collector. However, through some strange mystery they never succeeded. It was as if the Head-Collector would appear at will and vanish without a trace. Such is the known around Point Hope, Connecticut.

Brant had often heard the stories from the older locals of the town. Rumors of paranormal occurrences to vanishing suspects. As if they were to disappear without a trace and could never be found in other cities or towns outside of Point Hope. Point Hope was like a vacuum to them or a black hole, whichever the locals prefer. Harper never delved into the stories of the locals as deep as the other officers. He was always focused on the cases. Completing the task and going into the next case. Every so often would he hear the tales spoken by his colleagues of strange activities happening across the town. Some even suggested the crimes in New Haven were more tolerable than the strangeness hovering over Point Hope.

"I'll never get over the stories of this town. The people here, they truly believe there's something otherworldly here. As if it dwells under the concrete streets and the green fields. Maybe they're right. Maybe not. However, it is none of my concern. Only this case is."

Still sitting at the desk for several hours, studying every photo and document on the Head-Collector, Brant paused on one of the pages. Discovering an address. The details under the address stated the location was the home of the Head-Collector. Rumored to have been abandoned over ten years ago. Harper nodded and stamped the address, keeping a record of it. Brant collected the pages and photos and closed the folder. Leaning back in his chair and exhaling with relief as the touch of tiredness encompassed him.

"Tomorrow. Tomorrow, I'll head out to the home of this Head-Collector."

2

The next morning Brant awoke and began work on the case. Traveling out into the outskirts of Point Hope to the address. The drive was long. Even he wasn't aware as to how deep Point Hope rested in the midst of the wilderness. When you're in the town, everything seems open. As if the land is cleared for the view. Yet, when you're outside of the town, everything feels as if it's all closing around you. Like a door you can't fight. A looming shadow overlapping the solid figure in which it's made.

Within a twenty-minute drive, Brant looked ahead and could see a chimney. He knew it was the house as the map indicated the path of the address. Coming closer as the trees began to move past him as he drove closer, he could see the house. An old wooden home. Two floors. Stopping the car in front of the home. Brant exited. Seeing around him old barrels of wood laying around the ground. The grass buried under the covering of melting snow. Taking steps closer to the stairs of the porch. The scent of charred wood swift past him. The direction of its origin was unsure to Brant as he questioned the possibly of someone being inside the old home.

"No vehicles. No sign of any transportation of any kind. Strange. Yet common here."

Stepping onto the stairs of the porch. Brant walked until he heard the breaking of a branch behind him. Pausing, Brant turned quickly with his handgun raised toward the cause of the noise. Only to find himself staring at a man dressed in old rags and ripped clothing. The man held his hands up in fear of the gun. Brant sighed, slowly lowering the weapon. Not a complete lowering.

"I didn't know there was someone out here." The man said. "I heard the sound of a car and I came quickly to see who it could be."

"Do you live out here? Do you live in this home?"

"I live out here. Just not inside that home. It is a place of dread. Many people have died inside those old wooden walls."

"How are you aware of that?"

"Because. It is the home of the Head-Collector."

Brant nodded. It was indeed the Head-Collector's home. Just as the address indicated.

"Do you know if he's inside?" Brant asked. "Is the Head-Collector inside this home right now?"

"I do not know."

"Well. Can you tell me what I should know. I'm U.S. Marshal and Homicide Detective Brant Harper. I'm out here on a case. A case to find the Head-Collector and end his trail of blood from continuing."

The man's eyes widen as he pointed toward Brant.

"You. You're the man who stopped the Pleasure Man."

"I see my work goes around. Didn't realize people outside of Point Hope would be aware."

"You shouldn't be here. We shouldn't be here."

"Why not? Because of the Head-Collector?"

"No. The owner of this land."

"The land? Who owns the land?"

"She does."

"I'm sorry." Brant said, shaking his head with confusion. "Who is she?"

"The Lady Abigail."

"Lady Abigail? I've never heard of a Lady Abigail. Does she live around here?"

"Yes. But, I would advise you not to go to her home. Many have done such a thing and have never returned."

"She's another murderer. Probably a helping hand to the Head-Collector. Where is this woman's home?"

"You should not go there. You should leave. Return to Point Hope. Remain there."

"I have a job to do. First, I need to know if the Head-Collector's inside. I'll deal with this Lady Abigail later."

"No one's been here in weeks. Maybe months."

"So, you don't know why there's the stench of burning wood out here?"

"Many places burn wood during the winter months. It's commonplace."

"Out in the middle of nowhere." Brant said with a straight face.

"They're people out here. In places."

"Where are they?"

"They're around. Most don't walk outside the boundaries of their homes often."

"How come?"

"They abide by Lady Abigail's laws. She is their leader. She protects them when in need."

"Seems she didn't do much of a job with the Pleasure Man. Best leave the protecting to the authorities. It helps some better."

"I'm not trying to bother you, Marshal. But, you're on her land. She would not want you here. No matter if you are working a case or not."

Brant became annoyed by the man's words. Not a sense of seriousness in him he thought. Brant placed his gun back into the holster, turning away from the man as he focused on the home. The man yelled like a wounded dog as he stepped forward. Brant turned back to the man whit his gun on his side.

"What?" Brant asked with a hint of anger.

"Do not go in there." The man said. "It's not safe."

"I have a job to do, sir. I expect to see it through."

"Don't! Lady Abigail will not be pleased of your trespass."

"Sir. Leave me to my business or else I'll take you in for custody."

The man went silent. His face emotionless. With a slight nod of the head, the man turned and walked away from the home. Brant watched as the man left and somewhat vanished through the snow-covered trees into the wilderness. The man didn't even bother to walk on the road to have a better view of his path. It seemed strange to Brant. However, he turned back toward the home and approached the front door. He knocked three times and waited for a answer. Nothing. Brant held his gun tightly as he went to open the door. Only to find it locked. A sigh came from Brant's mouth as he stepped back, kicking the door open. The swing of the door echoed through the home and the outside. Brant stood still as the stench of blood poured out of the home. To the point where Brant had to cover his noise to avoid the smell.

"He was here. This is his place."

Brant entered the home, hearing only the sounds of creaking beneath his feet. Taking a thorough search through the home. On the first floor, Brant found nothing but old furniture, broken utensils, and used cigarettes. A filthy home to dwell in. Brant was disgusted by the scenery. Looking at the staircase, Brant walked slowly up the stairs. Seeing three rooms ahead. He searched them with ease. Two rooms had no furniture. They were simply empty. The third room had a bed. Worn out from time. Stains of a sort rested on the sheets and pillows. Even the room itself had a smell of its own. As if water flowed through the room without a break. It reminded Brant of the gym and shower in his academy days. Finding nothing worth of evidence on the second floor, Brant returned to the first. Taking the turn toward the back of the home, Brant was surprised to see the wooden floors with specks of blood. Brant knelt down. Wiping the blood with a piece of tissue from his jacket pocket.

"Droplets fell here."

Brant looked and noticed a pattern of the blood. Moving in a line toward the backdoor of the home. Approaching the backdoor, he opened it with his gun raised. Standing in the backyard as the ground is covered in snow. He knew no one had been there due to the amount of snow. Nearly three feet in height from the ground. What Brant did notice was the smell of decay near him. Looking around for the origin of the smell. He realized the snow near the gate was higher than usual. A chance Brant took by removing the snow with his own hands as he could not find a shovel to dig. As the snow fell, the stench grew stronger. Once he moved enough snow, Brant stumbled back as he saw what was causing the odor.

"Ah shit." Brant said with a quickening setback.

Brant stood still. Gazing down at a decaying deer. A large buck. What was strange about the animal's body was it had no head. By the look of it, Brant could tell the head was chopped off. The wound on the body was a clean cut. Whomever had decapitated the deer knew how to cut perfectly. Brant took the notice as pure evidence of the Head-Collector's presence being in the area. This was enough evidence of the home belonging to the Head-Collector.

"I'm getting closer. Closer than I thought I would in such a quick

amount of time. Point Hope is a small place. I only thought it would take some more digging for me to discover more."

3

Returning to his home, Brant went back to the map of Point Hope and the wilderness around. Going from the home which he had just returned from and moving the pen down a trail. Leading deeper into the forest. Brant knew there was something deep within the woods. Perhaps it was the dwelling place of the Lady Abigail the wanderer warned him about. However, Brant noticed the Head-Collector's movements across the map. Each path led him closer to the exit of the town. If the Head-Collector were to escape Point Hope without being caught, he would be in the boundaries of New Haven. Something Brant could not let happen. With no other options available for Brant to take upon. He took a moment of thought.

"This Lady Abigail. I wonder. I wonder if she's aware of the Head-Collector's workings throughout the area. Within the town. I must ask her."

Brant gathered the files and headed out into the woods once more. Now on the trail leading into the unknown. While driving, he noticed the same homeless man wandering around the road. The man waved as Brant slowed down.

"You again." Brant said.

"You aren't going to her home are you?"

"Why not? I believe she may know something about the Head-Collector."

"Do not trespass on her home. She will bring forth dark forces to take you out."

"Dark forces? What are you talking about?"

"She's not as you think. She isn't ordinary. She's beyond our understanding."

"Either way, I need answers. She may have them."

"Please, Detective." The man begged. "Do not go there. No one ever returns!"

Brant stared at the man and could sense he was honest about his words. He nodded.

"I have to try." Brant said with a calm voice.

Brant drove away as the homeless man watched on as Brant's car took a left turn, heading down the path toward the home of The Lady Abigail. The homeless man shook his head. Not in shame. But in despair as what Brant will encounter. Down the trail, a long trail, Brant drove. Nothing but trees on every side. Only the front and back are clear aside from the snow-covered grounds and the whistling cold air. The trail seemed to grow longer by the moments as Brant drove. Looking somewhat at an endless road into the unknown. Behind him appeared the same.

"Where is this place?"

Driving up, Brant noticed an end to the trees on the sides. Once past them, his eyes caught the sight of a castle. A large castle. Such castles aren't known to the people of Point Hope. Perhaps even to those in New Haven and beyond. The castle appeared grim. Made with Victorian sculpture. The road led to the front of the castle grounds and Brant went ahead and drove toward it. Passing by an old vineyard and stable. No horses. No husbandmen or maids to tend the vines. Although Brant was aware of their uncertainty due to the wintry weather. The car stopped as Brant exited. Standing before the monument which was the castle.

"When the homeless man said a home, I didn't think he meant a castle."

Brant looked to his side, checking his firearm. Making sure it was loaded. He also carried a small blade attached to his pocket. In front of him were the stairs to the entrance of the castle. No gate Brant thought to himself. No matter, he went ahead up the staircase, approaching the large double-doors without a hint of concern as to what may be on the other side. Brant stopped at the doors and saw their height. Standing nearly twelve feet in length. He knocked. Waiting for a response. After the second time knocking, Brant looked toward the windows. Seeing if he can get a peek. Once he reached the nearest window, he couldn't see anything due to the blinds within and the painted murals which were upon the windows.

"This place is old. Very old."

Brant wondered if the castle had any phone service. Seeing how there weren't any phone lines of any kind in the area where the castle stood. Returning to the door to knock once again. His hand raised as the doors themselves creaked open. Causing Brant to pause in his place as he watched the doors grant him entrance.

"I see."

Brant walked into the castle as the doors closed behind him with an elegance. Brant looked forward, seeing the red carpet glinting by the daylight. The murals brightened with their colors of emerald and ruby. The walls and ceiling appeared as solid gold with a slight scorch. The sight was impressive to someone like Brant who's never been in a place such as this. Nor in a land where a castle would be standing.

"Is there anyone here? Anyone besides me?"

Brant walked into the lounge room where he saw several couches and recliner chairs sitting alongside a fireplace. There were a fire. Brant knew something wasn't right about the castle. How can there be a fire when they're no one home? Or so he assumed by the image of seeing no one during his entrance. Brant continued his walk as he took a seat in one of the chairs facing the fireplace. While sitting, a quick touch of air rubbed his neck. The touch felt as if ice was placed on him. The feeling caused him to turn around with a quickness. He knew something or someone was inside with him.

"Who's here?" Brant asked. "Show yourself."

At the entrance where Brant walked in, he caught a glimpse of a shadow. A shadow cloaked in darkness. From that moment, Brant stood up and took out his firearm. Walking near the sight of the shadow figure. Turning to the corridor on the right side of the entrance, Brant saw nothing. No one. Only an empty hallway. He nodded and proceeded to walk into the hallway. Within the hallway, there were barely any light as the windows were small. Only a glimmer of sunlight could enter the hall for a better view. Knowing this, Brant took out his flashlight and walked down the hallway. Gun in one hand. Flashlight in the other. The air in the castle began to have a presence of its own. One Brant could feel as he stepped deeper into the hallway.

"Who's here?" Brant questioned. "I know there's someone in here."

Within the end of the hallway, Brant caught the image of a figure. Same cloaked in shadow. His gun raised ad flashlight pointing toward the figure, which unveiled its bodily presence. Yet it had no face. The hands were as pale as the falling snow. Nails blue as the sky.

"Who are you?" Brant asked. "Are you the Lady Abigail?"

The figure did not respond. Brant took several steps forward toward the figure. His gun steady as was the flashlight. He asked the same questions once more to another moment of silence from the figure of shadows. Brant became tired of the non-responsiveness. Proceeding to approach the figure, Brant lowered the gun and went to grab the figure's arm. Discovering his hand moving through it as if the figure were fog. To Brant's shocking expression, a creepy giggle exhaled from the figure as it vanished from his sight. Brant looked around the hallway to catch the figure. Only he was standing in the hallway by himself.

"What was that? Was that a ghost?"

Returning to the front. Brant noticed a change in furniture. The couches and chairs were switched in positions. Now all of them were facing their backs against the fireplace, which the fire was out. Only smoke reached above the burnt wood. A sound of wind moved through the home as he lights began to flicker. Raising his gun up, Brant went and stood against the wall as he had a good view of his surroundings.

"I am not afraid of you. Whatever you are. Now, I will ask once more? Where is the Lady Abigail?"

The intensity of the flickering lights increased as did the wind. The doors rattled in chaotic fashion as the furniture began to move on its own. Bouncing on and off the floor. The fire combusted once again in the fireplace, mixed with the smoke of the past. With all the commotion taking place, Brant was not afraid. He was ready to strike whatever was coming for him. As he could feel the presence of a figure within the castle. Its unseen eyes watching him from every corner. Ahead of him on the other end of the living room, the two doors open to Brant's surprise. Silence entered the living room. The furniture ceased. The doors paused. The fire steady.

"Show yourself." Brant commanded. "I'm wasting my time here."

Through the silence muffled the sound of footsteps. Echoing within the darkness of the opened doors. The steps of heels approached as through the shadowed entrance entered a woman. A peculiar one dressed in a black gown. Coated in white linings. Hair dark as crows. Lips as red as blood. Her eyes matched the emerald in the murals. Brant saw as she entered the living room and the doors behind her shut by themselves. In her left hand, she held a rose. Something which was seemly strange to Brant. The woman saw Brant and stared at him with a grin on her face.

"Are you the Lady Abigail?"

"I am. And who might you be? Aside from a trespasser in my home."

"I am Brant Harper." He said, walking toward her. "United States Marshal and Homicide Detective."

"And why has a detective come to my domain? Is there something here in which you desire?"

"Because I believe you may know something about the killer lurking around the area. The killer known as the Head-Collector."

Abigail's eyes widen with a much larger grin growing on her face. A small hunt of laughter exhaled from her lips. Brant stood in confusion at the scenery. It itched him.

"The Head-Collector's nowhere to be found. He died many ages ago."

"Ages ago? No. he is alive and well and is on the trail once more. I'm investigating his murders. He's still at large. Killing people. Decapitating them and collecting their heads. I need to know if you have some details I can gather to find him and end his spree."

"Detective Harper, let me give you some words in which you may understand or may not understand. The Head-Collector is nothing more than an urban tale told to the wrongdoers of this land. The town you know of as Point Hope is only a beacon to such stories.

Brant disagreed with Lady Abigail. He knew she possessed some knowledge on the Head-Collector and he was going to get it out of her by any means of interrogation.

"Ma'am. I'm sorry to have come to your home. A castle of all places. Here in Connecticut. It's something else. I must know if you're aware of anything related to the Head-Collector? Anything."

Abigail gave Brant a nod. He nodded back in reply. With a sigh breathing from her mouth, she took a seat in one of the recliner chairs. Taking out a pipe and smoking it. She exhaled slowly. Brant waited for an answer.

"Ms. Abigail, I'm sorry to rush you on your response. But, I do not have a lot of time. I need some information and I'll be on my way."

"Information you say?"

"Yes. On the Head-Collector. I need to know something that I may find him."

Abigail nodded as she exhaled once more. The smoke levitated through the living room, past Brant.

"And what will you do once you find the Head-Collector? Will you bring forth the justice the dead sought? Their loved ones seek? What will you do once you've achieved your mission?"

"I will bring him to the authorities, and he'll be placed in prison. Potentially for life. He'll no longer be able to harm those of the innocent."

Abigail laughed greatly to Brant's displeasure. The words he spoke were as dung to her ears. She exhaled as she clapped her hands together in the humor she heard in Brant's words.

"What is funny to you?"

"Your view of justice, detective. Your ideal methods of punishing those who have done harm. Such harm as murder cannot go unpunished."

"He'll be locked up in prison. He won' be able to harm anyone else. Justice is done."

"Is it? Or when the time comes, shall he be let loose to bring more harm onto the world? Shall he inspire others to continue his work. To become more than just a murderer. To become a god amongst men."

"You speak as if you're aware of his purpose for killing. That means you know something. Tell me now."

"Very well. The Head-Collector was once a student of this castle. This castle is not just my home. It is the dwelling place of many souls who have come and gone. This castle has been standing in the wilderness of this and for centuries. As have I."

Brant shook his head as he stepped back from Abigail's presence. Her words did not add up to him. Her eyes however told something different from the words which came forth from her lips. They were strange. Mysterious. Peculiar.

"You see, Detective. I must tell you. The things you encountered while inside my castle, they were no mirage. No illusions. It's real. All of it."

Through the doorways came forth more of the shadow figures. Brant turned and raised his gun to them. Seeing over a dozen of them surrounding the living room from every entry point. Abigail smiled as she saw them.

"What is this?"

"This is reality, detective. There are things in this world the masses have yet to encounter. Yet to believe."

"So what? Are these ghosts? Demons?"

"They're spirits. Spirits of the past. Souls that have been slaughtered to keep me alive."

"You killed people."

"Others did it for me. My servants. However, they're long gone. My last servant was the murderer you seek. For that reason of his loyalty to me, I cannot give him up. No matter his actions outside of my castle grounds."

"You've admitted to aiding a murderer. You're part of his crimes. For that reason, I must take you in to the authorities as well."

Brant stepped forward to grab Abigail's arm. Yet, while reaching one of the spirits rushed toward him. Standing between him and Abigail. The cold air touched Brant's face as Abigail grinned.

"I am not going anywhere."

Brant nodded, stepping back as his eyes were on Abigail and the shadow figures. His gun was raised.

"I don't want to shoot in here."

"Go ahead. Surprise me."

One of the shadows lunged toward him, Brant fried a shot and the shadow vanished. The others followed as Brant continued to shoot them to Abigail's pleasure. His eyes showed no fear as the shadow continued followed by Abigail's dark laughter in the distance. After the shots were fired, Abigail stood up and applauded Brant for his bravery. With a wave of her hand, the front doors opened, startling Brant as he looked back to them.

"Take your leave from my castle, detective. I give you this one blessing."

"I will report you to the authorities. They will come here and bring you in."

"I'll love to see them try."

Brant stepped back with his eyes on Abigail as he went for the doors. On his way out, Abigail called out to him. He turned back slightly with his hand ready to go for the gun.

"I give you this one warning. If I ever see you again on my grounds, I will set foot upon your little town of Point Hope and I will show the world what truly dwells beyond the scales of their eyes."

Brant nodded and exited the castle. The doors closed behind him as Abigail watched his every step down the staircase.

4

The next day, Brant arrived back the office in a hurry, barging into the Chief's office to his displeasure. Brant begged to explain himself as the Chief simply agreed to let him talk as the visitor who was sitting inside the office decided to leave. Giving the Chief a moment with one of his detectives. The door closed behind Brant as the Chief's full attention was on him.

"Now, what do you need to tell me?'

"It's about the case I'm working on."

"Which case besides the one I've placed everyone on?"

"The Head-Collector case."

The Chief sighed.

"Tell me, you did not go back inside that office and pick another file. I told you those are not meant for you or anyone else here. All those files are confidential. Nothing more. Nothing less."

"Sir, it is important. He's still on the loose and I've uncovered his trail. I know where he's going."

"Very well. Humor me on everything you've learned about this Collector?"

Brant nodded as he laid the file atop the Chief's desk and sat down in the seat. Opening the file for the Chief to get a look.

"Ever since I started on this case, it's led me to some disturbing places. Both physically and mentally."

"How disturbing are you talking?"

"Very disturbing. The first thing I learned what an abandoned home on the outskirts of town. Found nothing but a decapitated buck and a wanderer who told me the land belonged to some Lady Abigail."

"No way." The Chief chuckled.

"What is it?"

"Lady Abigail? This homeless guy told you to beware the Lady Abigail?"

"Yes," Brant paused. "Wait. How do you know?"

"Everyone in this town has heard the folktales of the Lady Abigail. A mysterious woman. Dressed in black who lives in an old castle within the wilderness of the land. She controls an army of shadow spirits. Ghosts basically under her thumb. It's an old wives' tale told to spook children and weak men alike."

Brant stayed quiet. A little too quiet for the Chief.

"You know something, don't you?"

"Sir, she's not a folktale. She's real."

The Chief sat up in his seat toward the desk. His eyes locked on Brant as he slid the file over to the side.

"Tell me how you know this."

"I saw her. I spoke with her. The castle is real. She is real."

"And you came back here alive? Huh. Just this one time, I'm impressed with you. Now, why go and bother the woman?"

"She knew about the Head-Collector. Said he was one of her students in the past. She knew where he was going."

"And where's he off to now?"

"New Haven." Brant said, pointing down toward the map on the desk.

The Chief sighed as he leaned back in the chair.

"Very well. If this Collector is heading off to New Haven, it is no longer your concern."

"But, sir. I'm onto this. I can stop him if I find him before he enters their jurisdiction."

"No need. Let the Marshals and detectives of New Haven handle this guy. Besides, some of their own problems have leaked into our territories."

"What's happened?"

"You're familiar with that Vigilante Congregation in New Haven. The one that was led by that infamous Hoyt Bennett?"

"I'm aware."

"Well, those bastards have come here. Into our town. A few of them at least. From what we've learned from the New Haven branch, remnants from the Congregation have fled into our land, seeking a place to dwell before they leave for Hoyt's return."

"Is that why all the officers here are on alert?"

"That's right and I need you to work this case. They'll need you on this one. Every hand-on-deck at the most."

"Chief, there's plenty of officers and detectives that can handle a few renegades from New Haven. Let me find this killer before he enters New Haven and brings forth more trouble for them than this Hoyt Bennett ever did."

The Chief disagreed with Brant's proposal to remain on the case. Instead, the Chief continued to tell him to lead the other officers on the trail for the remnants of the Congregation. Brant sighed in annoyance, taking the file and exiting the office as the Chief continued on about leaving the Head-Collector to the detectives of New Haven. Walking out in the lobby, Brant watched as the other officers headed out in mass to search out the Congregation's followers. Brant followed them outside to the vehicles. Entering his own, he made his leave. Taking an alternate route than the officers. Brant wasn't concerned about a small group of men from New Haven. Hs concern was the Head-Collector and him alone.

Driving out near the area where Interstate 95 rested, Brant followed on a small note of information which he discovered buried within the file toward the back. The details indicated a small cabin deep in the woods near the interstate. It seemed like the perfect spot for a killer to make his escape and Brant knew it for sure. Driving down the open road similar to the road near the castle, this time Brant saw the cabin ahead and it was clear. There was no other vehicle besides his own. Exiting the car at the gated entrance, Brant scouted the location for anyone. Including the Head-Collector. Brant believed the killer could be hiding inside the cabin, planning his move to escape.

"Seems like there's no one here. Dammit."

Brant went to open the door until the sound of rustling came from the trees behind him. Near the entrance onto the cabin grounds. Brant took out his firearm and walked steady near the sight of the sound. Seeing no one, yet hearing the cracking of wood in the distance, Brant yelled out orders to come out from the woods and face him. Hearing the branches crack coming closer, exiting the woods were two Caucasian men. Dressed in jeans and jackets. One had a beard. The other was clean-shaven. Brant didn't recognize them, yet they appeared to have been on the run due to their dirty attire.

"Who are you guys?" Brant asked.

"We're just passing through. That's all." The bearded man said.

"Hey, this cabin yours?" The clean-shaven man asked. "I'm curious because if it isn't, perhaps my friend and I can use it while we're here. For just a rest stop."

"First off, this cabin isn't mine. It belongs to a killer. Second, both of you will stay put until you answers my questions."

"Questions? What are we? Arrested or something?"

"Where are you both from?"

"We come from New Haven. Just looking for a place to stay while our homes are being renovated."

"You decided to come into Point Hope because your homes are being renovated?"

"Yeah."

Brant shook his head.

"I'm not buying that shit."

"Look man, we're not trying to cause trouble or anything. We just need a place to stay. After our situation back in New Haven is settled, we'll be out of this land before you can say stop, drop, and roll."

Brant sighed. His gun still aimed toward the two strangers.

"One more question then."

"Go for it."

"We you part of the Congregation?"

"I'm sorry?" The bearded man said.

"You heard what I said. Were either of you part of the Congregation? The one led by Hoyt Bennett?"

The two men stood paused. Their eyes moving back and forth between themselves.

"Answer my question and I'll let you go."

"Afraid we can't do that!" The bearded man said, raising up his gun.

Before he could take a shot Brant fired his own, shooting both men in the head. The brief moment of silence cleared the air after the echoed gunfire. Brant sighed with displeasure as more footsteps were sounded from the woods. Listening closely, Brant could hear the voices of more men. He knew they were part of the Congregation as well. Once they stepped out from the trees, Brant saw them. Nearly over a dozen of them. Wielding firearms of their own. Dressed in jeans and big coats. The first ones looked down at the bodies of their comrades.

"Who did this?" Their leader spoke.

"Must be those guys from back home. They've followed us here."

"Nah. I'll see that to be true once they arrive. Right now, this was the cause of someone here. Perhaps they're inside that cabin."

Looking around, they saw Brant's car. Brant looked out from the cabin window, seeing them approaching the car.

"Shit."

Brant bolted from the cabin door with his gun raised. Gaining the attention of the Congregation. Their leader looked, seeing Brant standing at the cabin door.

"Did you kill my brethren?"

"They brought it on themselves. Now, why don't you guys take your leave and return to New Haven. This land is under the jurisdiction of Point Hope. You don't belong here."

The leading vigilante scoffed at Brant's words.

"You believe we're just going to let you live after you killed two of our own in cold blood? I don't think so."

The leader commanded his men to take fire at Brant. Their firearms raised just as Brant jumped back inside the cabin. The guns go off, blasting into the cabin. Brant moved the furniture around to hide as the bullets pierce through the wood. Brant kept his head ducked, hearing their leader shouting over the gunfire to bring vengeance upon him. Looking around toward the back, Brant saw a door and rushed to exit the cabin. Running through the gunfire and blasting himself through the back door, he found himself back on the outside. The Congregation could not see him as the cabin covered him. He sighed and turned around toward the trees. Only to see six individuals standing before him. Dressed in black and Kevlar. Carrying firearms. Four men and two women. The man in the middle stepped forward as the gunshots continued.

"Are you with them?" Brant asked.

"We're here to stop them."

"And who are you guys?"

"We're United States Marshals. From New Haven. These guys are our concern."

"I'll help you guys."

"No need." The man said. "Let us do our work."

"You don't understand. I'm a U.S. Marshal as well. From Point Hope. I'm here on a case and these men surrounded me after I killed two of their own."

"I see. Very well. Continue with your case. Leave these guys to us."

"Mind if I get your name?"

"Preston Maddox. Now go."

Maddox and his team of Emily Weston, Cody Aries, Darius Conway, Gloria Hunter, and newcomer Leon Thompson walked past Brant toward the cabin, taking looks out toward the Congregation. As they prepared themselves, Brant looked over to his left, seeing the bodies of the two men he killed being pulled into the forest.

"The hell?"

Brant ran after the bodies. Meanwhile, Preston and his team prepared themselves as the gunfire ceased. Loading their weapons. Unlike the others, Cody carried a sniper rifle and Leon wielded a bow and arrow. A weapon he preferred in the field.

"Didn't expect to find other Marshals out here." Preston said. "For what? I'm not concerned."

"Never knew there were Marshals in Point Hope." Cody mentioned. "Town's so small for one I suppose."

"How's it looking?" Preston asked.

Cody took a look, seeing the Congregation regrouping as they slowly approached the cabin.

"They're on their way to the cabin. Any second now."

"Any adjustments?" Darius asked.

"No. Terminate the Congregation. Clear Hoyt's residue. That's the mission. Eldon expects us to finish this."

"Very well then." Leon said, holding an arrow. "Let's have some fun with this."

Preston nodded.

"Everyone take your positions."

Preston looked over to Emily, seeing her with no expression on her face. A sheer moment of solemn came over him.

"Are you sure you can go through with this?" Preston asked.

"I'm here aren't I."

"Yeah." Preston nodded.

Preston turned the corner, gaining the attention of the Congregation.

"Take your shots!"

The shootout commenced as Preston fire toward the vigilantes in front of him. On the other end of the cabin, Darius and Gloria took their shots. Atop the cabin, Cody laid low, sniping vigilantes near the tree line as Leon fired arrows through their legs and arms. The vigilante leader looked out toward the cabin from behind the trees, seeing Preston and Emily in particular taking fire toward them.

"It's them. The same ones who put our leader behind bars."

Preston and Emily reached the front of the cabin, taking out the vigilantes with ease. On the other end, Darius and Gloria approached, standing beside Preston and Emily as they fired.

"How many are left?" Darius questioned.

"It's like there's no end to them." Gloria said.

"As many until there are none." Preston said.

Seeing a clearing of vigilantes standing, the Marshals continued to finish off the remaining ones. Once the area was silent, the leader stepped forward. Holding two shotguns in his hand.

"You can't take us out. Hoyt will be free again and his vision will come to pass."

"I'm afraid not." Preston said.

The shotguns clicked as Preston took the shot, killing the leader. The snow covered in bodies, bullets, and blood as Preston and the Marshals circled the area.

"Hope that's the last of them." Cody said.

"As do I." Preston replied.

5

Hearing the faint gunfire, Brant continued to chase down the two bodies of the Congregation as they were pulled through the woods. Following the trails of blood in the snow, Brant moved quicker than he had done before. Nearly reaching the end of the wood line, Brant stumbled out of the woods to find no bodies. Only the fact he was standing in a cul-de-sac of a suburban neighborhood. Confusion grew on his face. How could the wilderness where the castle stands be so close to a neighborhood? Brant didn't take the moment to think.

"They're inside one of these homes."

Brant went and checked the homes. There were ten of them in the neighborhood. Built the same. Outer structure were exact copies. Brant searched the homes for blood and didn't find any. Neither was there any sign of blood in the snow. While walking toward one of the last three homes, a stench caught his attention. A smell similar to what he found in the abandoned home.

"Blood."

Brant turned to his left as he walked in the center of the road, staring at a home. The stench increased as he approached the front door. Grabbing the door handle, the door was locked. Brant scoffed as he stepped back, kicking in the door and rushing in with his gun aimed.

"What died in here?"

Brant covered his nose from the odor, which was stronger than it appeared outside. The musk of the air was dosed in blood and water. He searched the home, finding nothing related to his cause. While walking near the back door, Brant turned to his right and noticed sitting next to him was a set of stairs which led into the basement. Brant believed it would be the spot to find the bodies. Stepping down on the stairs, the smell grew stronger. Reaching the floor of the basement, the dim light bulb was already on, giving Brant something to keep an eye on. The ground was wet from melted snow and flowing through the water was the sight of blood. Brant knew he was in the right place. Looking around the basement, Brant saw a refrigerator sitting against the wall. Opening the refrigerator as the cold air burst toward him. What Brant saw caused him to freeze for a moment.

"The hell?"

Looking into the refrigerator, Brant saw the head of the deer he found at the home as well as other heads from victims. He shut the door out of panic. Taking a second before opening up the freezer at the top and seeing the two severed heads of the vigilantes he killed. Brant shut the freezer door and breathed.

"This is his place. He's here."

"You're right. I am." A low voice said behind Brant.

With a quick turnaround, Brant stood and saw him. The Head-Collector himself. Shrouded by the darkness of the room with his face hidden by his dark brown fedora. His body hidden with his long trench-coat. The Head-Collector's hands rested in his coat pockets. Brant raised up his gun, ready to take the shot.

"I've been looking for you."

"I know. And you've come to take me in."

"I am. You're under arrest for the murders you've committed."

The Head-Collector chuckled.

"I'm not going to the authorities. I'm beyond such laws of man."

"You're just a man." Brant said. "You're under the jurisdiction of Point Hope, Connecticut. Thereby, you're coming with me."

"You really don't understand the reality of such things. Do you, boy."

"I'm not wasting anymore time. I've found you and I'm taking you in."

"Just like you did with the Pleasure Man? Do worry yourself. I know all about your past case. Saving the family from such a treacherous man. A pity he died the way he did. Hopeless. Without anyone there to help him see the terror in his ways."

"Terror in his ways? What you're saying surely doesn't fit the things you've done. Killing people and animals. Keeping their heads in your collection like trophies."

"They are trophies. Accomplishments of my work."

Brant coughed with disgust.

"Part of me is saying I should just kill you and end this."

"Well then, what's taking you so long. You have two options set before you. Take me down and bring me to the authorities or kill me and end my journey of hunting."

"I can't just choose from those choices. This is life and death we're talking about."

"By that case, I will make the choice for you."

From the Head-Collector's right hand, he reached into his coat and pulled out a machete. Smeared in the blood of his victims. Brant's eyes caught it by the glinting of the light.

"Let's see what you're really made of, Brant Harper."

With a quick jump and lunge, the Head-Collector swiped hematite near Brant, stepping back to avoid the attacks, Brant ducked and dodged the blood-covered blade as the Head-Collector laughed after every attack. Moving around the table, Brant used it to duck and jump past the machete swipes. Ducking past the coming slash, Brant turned around and shot the Head-

Collector in the shoulder. The machete dropped as the Head-Collector shouted in pain and in anger.

"Oh, you've done it now, boy."

Picking up the machete with his left hand, the Head-Collector smashed the light bulb. Causing the basement to be shrouded in darkness. Brant, unable to see what's happening, hears footsteps going up the staircase. Finding the stairs with the help of his flashlight, Brant ran up to the first floor as he caught the snippet of the Head-Collector bolting through the front door. Running outside, Brant chased the Head-Collector down the road. Every step became heavier due to the amount of snow which was built up. The Head0Collector rushed into the woods and Brant followed. Brant ran and ran until he heard the sound of vehicles on the road. Stepping out of the woods to find himself on Interstate 95 with a sign pointing in the location of New Haven. Brant looked around and there was no sign of the Head-Collector. A sigh of anger exhaled from his mouth.

"He's entered their jurisdiction. I can't. I can't stop him now. Shit."

With the Head-Collector vanishing from the area and no one else to track down, Brant made his return back to the cabin, finding the landscape empty with only blood in the snow. No bodies. While walking to his car, Preston waited fro him. Startling him for a bit.

"No need to get scared."

"Thought I was the only one out here. Where did your partners go?"

"Back to New Haven to bring forth the news. The Vigilante Congregation is no more. What of your mission?"

"Mission failed."

"How so?"

"My target is no longer in my jurisdiction. He's on his way

into New Haven."

Preston nodded.

"Huh. I see. So, what will you do now?"

"I'm not sure. I can speak with my chief. See if he gives me permission to work in New Haven. Track down this killer."

"How about this. Since New Haven is my territory and you're saying there's a killer on the loose. Let my boss speak with your chief. Make an arrangement to get you working out there."

"That's possible?"

"You must be young in this field. I understand. Yes, it is possible."

Brant sighed with relief. Nodding.

"Thank you. I don't know what else to say."

"Once you arrive in New Haven, contact the Marshal service there. I'll like to tag along with you on this one."

"Are you sure? This killer might be a handful."

"I've dealt with my share of killers. One from Point Hope won't be much of a difference."

"How are you so sure of that?"

"Call it an *Instinct*."

LOST IN SHADOWS: REMASTERED EXCERPT

1

New Haven Detective and U.S. Marshal Preston Maddox drives down a pair of narrow streets as he's on the search for Jonny Cartel, one of the top drug lords of New Haven, Connecticut. Preston, who's wearing his casual suit attire, drives through the quiet streets of New Haven. He turns a corner that heads toward Orange Avenue, around the West River.

"I take it he's around this area. Somewhere."

He turned a corner, which was leading him into a dark pathway. On the other side of the street is a small warehouse covered in rusted panels. Preston drove closer to the warehouse and spotted a white van on the left side. Preston noticed a group of guys standing by the van, wearing all black with their faces barely covered, stacking what appears to be bags of marijuana and cocaine in the back. Preston also noticed a black SUV beside the van with one man coming out, wearing a white suit with slick hair.

"There's the son of a bitch." Preston said as he sees Jonny Cartel.

Preston slowly put the car in park and turned off the vehicle. He exited out of the car and began walking toward the scene. As he walked closer, one of the men spotted him and started yelling. The other men looked up and see Preston. Jonny turned and stared at Preston. Preston does the same.

"Well, looks like the Instinct has found me." Jonny said. "What's the next step, Detective? I hope you're not here for a license plate or sticker check on my SUV here."

"I'm here to take your worthless self to prison. Unless you have another option of a location you'll like to take you?"

Jonny laughed as he looked toward his men. They laughed along with him, until Preston glared at them. Jonny turned back to Preston, looking at his clothes before keeping his attention focused on Preston.

"Look here, I got an hour before I leave for Miami. So, do me a favor, Maddox. Get a change in style of clothes for once. This whole intimidation approach isn't quite working for you when you're wearing only slacks and a casual jacket."

"I appreciate your generosity in the apparel department, Cartel. Though, I can care less on how you perceive someone's clothing. Anyway, that's not why I'm here and you know why I'm here standing before you and your pack of goons."

"OK, so what can I do to change your mind? Hmm? Give you some profit on the side? Hand you one of my nice fine women to keep you company for the time being?"

"I can care less about your greenbacks or your filthy whores you have stashed back at your place."

Preston held his ground quietly.

"I'm giving you a few choices to make. Either you can come with me, get in my car and I'll ship you off to prison or we can have ourselves a classic standoff where you and most of your men here are killed on the spot. Your decision, not mine."

Jonny stood quietly, not making a sound. Only staring at Preston. Preston kept his eyes locked on Cartel, not making any facial expressions of any kind.

"Tongue turned to lead, Cartel?"

Jonny walked toward the van. He tells his men to pack up

whatever they had in their hands and told them to leave the area. The men toss whatever they have into the van and they drive it off into the darkness of street. Preston and Jonny are the only two men at the warehouse.

"Alright, Maddox. Now you have a choice to make and make it right for yourself."

"OK. What are these choices you have in mind for myself that would make me accept them and leave you here to continue your pathetic way?'

Jonny moved his right hand to his side, revealing a revolver under the side of his jacket. Preston noticed it and looked up at Jonny.

"You sure you want to play this little round? I told you already. You want to go that route, you'll end up dead and possibly some of your men too."

"There is no other way around all of this. Now, you can choose your choice. Either you can go ahead and leave this area and don't make a second thought or I could just shoot you on the spot and leave your body to rot."

"So, if I choose the first one, I assume I'll live. If I take the second option, you're going to put one in me. Is that how this is going here?"

"You're smarter than how you dress yourself, Marshal."

"Funny. The decisions you've just gave me are similar to the choices that you gave to that woman I suppose."

Jonny stood frozen still, having what appeared to be a confused and worried look on his face. He shook his head before staying still.

"I'm afraid I don't know what you're talking about, Marshal."

"The woman, whose body was found in the river a few weeks ago. I know you're aware of the case. Only her torso was found floating in the water. Her lower body was discovered across town at some cannibal site where they were partially eating off of it. They eat mostly the thighs and some of the calves. Other than that, they still left some over for anyone to share."

"Holy shit Holy shit! God damn it! If you knew how she behaved and how she acted, you would know deep down that she deserved it, *Instinct*!.."

"No, I don't know why. Probably will never figure out why you had her killed and fed to cannibals. But, overall, why did she deserve it? Is it because she didn't have enough federal reserve notes to pay her remaining price off?"

"She was nothing but a traitorous whore. Sneaking behind my back, working for that Ray Colby guy from Jersey since he just opened ship down here in my town. My town! That kind of shit doesn't play fair in my world of business, Maddox and you understand that don't you."

"I do. But, its none of my concern how you run your business. My concern is stopping your business and putting you in a cell or maybe six feet under."

Jonny started to shake, he held up the revolver, pointed at Preston. Preston stood still, starting at Cartel.

"You know what, I've just had enough of this! I have a plane to catch, Marshal. Big business meeting tomorrow. So, if you'll excuse me."

Jonny started walking toward the SUV. Preston stood his ground, with his right hand to his side. Jonny, still pointing the revolver, gets to the driver's seat of the SUV. Preston stared at Jonny with his hand still to his side. Jonny paused and shut the door as he started stomping toward Preston with the revolver.

"You take one step, you son of a bitch and I'm going to blow your fucking brains out all over this place, Instinct!"

"I wouldn't try that, Cartel. You wouldn't want to make a

big mistake by killing a United States Marshal and ruining your world of business for a very long time to come. Even if you have a plane to catch for a supposed big business meeting. I'm sure your other clients and partners will understand what you've been through and will find a way for their business to continue in their eyes before they're caught on their own soil."

"I'll spell this out for you once and only this once. The only way I'll ever lose this business is OVER MY COLD, DECAYING, CORPSE!!!"

Preston pulled out his gun and fired shots toward Jonny in the chest a consecutive three times. Jonny slowly fell to the ground, dropping the revolver in the process. Preston walked toward Jonny, who's trying to reach for revolver while lying on the concrete pavement., Preston kicked it away from Jonny's hand. Jonny bled from his chest as his blood flowed around his body, soaking his suit.

"From the look of you on the ground holding your chest, you didn't listen to my warning, Cartel. I told you not to try anything like that."

"It doesn't matter, Marshal. Maybe I deserved to die. Maybe this is where my journey ends and all. But, soon, there will come a time where you are on the opposite end of a gunshot such as this and you'll be on the ground gasping for your breath. When the day comes that it happens, you'll know what's to come afterwards."

"I highly doubt your kind and strong prophetic words." Preston said with a smile. "But, whenever that day does arrive, I'll be in this same position and the other will be in the position that you're currently lying in."

Preston reached into his pocket, pulling out his black and silver Blackberry. He dialed 9-1-1. The phone started ringing and the 9-1-1 Operator is on the other end.

"9-1-1. Please state your immediate emergency."

"This is Preston Maddox. U.S. Marshal and secondary detective over at the New Haven Detective and Marshal Agency. I've called because I'm currently standing around the West River, close to Orange Avenue at a warehouse. I need an ambulance and a coroner right away."

"An ambulance is on its way, Marshal. Should I assist backup as well?"

"No need for that ma'am. Just the ambulance and coroner will do just fine. I appreciate it and thank you."

He hung up and placed the smartphone back into his pocket. He walked over to Jonny. He kneeled in front of him as Cartel continued to gasp for his breath.

"Don't worry, Jonny. Ambulance is on its way. They'll do what they can for your sake."

"What about the coroner? Don't think I didn't hear that part."

"That's just in case you die here. Which is the most probability."

"Just go to hell, Marshal. Go to hell and burn for the rest of your eternal days."

Jonny's head cocked over as he exhaled his last breath. Jonny died on the spot as Preston only stared at his deceased body. He nodded and walked back to his car, leaving Jonny on the ground for the ambulance to find.

In a suburban neighborhood lies many homes of which families and friends live among each other. One of the homes has its lights on and inside of the home's kitchen is a forty-year old mother washing the dishes as her sixteen-year-old daughter sat in the living room in front of a fireplace watching the TV.

"What are you watching over there?"

"Just some random show. Nothing much on tonight, so I figured I would just watch something that grabbed my interest."

"Seems to me how you're pretty quiet over there that you're either in deep of the show or your bored by it."

"It's interesting so far, mom."

The daughter turned and looked toward the door. Hearing a tapping sound coming from outside. Noticing that the room is quiet except for the TV and her mother washing the dishes. She sat up from off the couch and walked slowly close to the door to see if the sound was coming from outside. The sound started again, this time alerting the mother. She looked over and turned to her daughter, who continued to approach the door.

"What was that outside?"

"I'm not sure. Sound like its right next to the door. Do you want me to go ahead and check it out?"

"Since you're already on your feet, I suggest you could. Just be cautious. There's no telling what that sound could be. Especially in a city like this."

The sound faded away as the daughter inched closer to the door. The mother continued washing the dishes as she glanced over toward her daughter and looked at what was playing on the TV. Hearing no sound, she looked at her daughter.

"Everything alright over there? You seem to be a little nervous?"

"I'm doing fine. Just taking precautions, that's all."

The daughter placed her hand on the doorknob and slowly turned the knob. Opening the door slightly, it gives a chilling creak as she opened the door. Upon seeing nothing or no one by the door, she releases a sigh of relief. The mother walked over toward the living room, seeing her daughter looking out the door and she went back to the kitchen.

"Haley, is everything alright? What are you doing?"

"I'm-"

As she responded to her mother, a hand covered by a black glove quickly reached in from the open creak on the left side of the door. The hand snatched Haley by her jaw and held her mouth shut. She tried to release a scream to gain her mother's attention. Hearing a series of bumping sounds coming from the front, the mother dried her hands and walked out of the kitchen.

"What in the hell are you doing in here?"

She stood in a frozen state as she saw Haley fighting off the black glove. Haley trued kicking out of the door at the individual's body, but the black glove held Haley tightly and slammed her head into the wall. Her mother stood covering her mouth with tears beginning to flow from her eyes.

"Oh my god. Haley, I'm coming."

As she took a step, another black glove reached out from behind her as it appeared the individual came through the back door nearby the kitchen. The intervals entered the home, their bodies appeared to be fit, wearing all black with their faces covered with solid black masks, to where even their eyes aren't revealed. The two individuals throw Haley and her mother against the walls and begin to pummel them to the floor. Both scream for help as they're being beaten.

2

Officers arrived at a suburb home in the New Haven neighborhoods. They are heading through, going back and forth in and out of the home. An ambulance and coroner arrived on the scene as well. The paramedics entered the home with a stretcher, as do the coroner. A black car pulled up and out came Preston. He walked toward a fellow officer. The officer turned and was immediately what some would call star struck.

"U.S. Marshal and fellow New Haven detective, Preston Maddox." The Officer said. "It's an honor to meet you."

"It's an honor to meet you as well. So, what's the situation here, officer?"

"We received a call from one of the neighbors that something suspicious was occurring late last night at this house. From what we know, there were two females, one adult, the other, teenager. It seems that they were both murdered."

"Just being curious here, but, how were they murdered."

"I'll show you.' the Officer said. 'Follow me."

Preston followed the officer into the home. Inside, the home looked like your typical standard suburb home. A nice leather couch in the living room with a flat-screen TV, a beautiful kitchen with nice shiny tiles on the floor. The home currently filled and surrounded with officers, coroner, and forensic scientists. Preston looked inside the kitchen, to the left and seen the adult woman lying on the tile floor with her head severed.

Preston turned and said to the officer, "So, this is the mother. Couldn't really tell from a distance."

"Yes sir, the teenager is in the laundry room. Follow me, Marshal."

They walked into the laundry room, which is on the left side of the kitchen. Preston looked inside and noticed something red leaking from the dryer. He looked over to the officer and pointed to the dryer.

"Wait. Hold on a quick second. Please do not tell me that she's in there?" He asked.

"Marshal, I'm afraid she is." the officer said.

Another officer walked in and opened the dryer. The door widely opened as an arm flopped out, covered and dripping with blood. They looked inside and see that the teenage girl was shoved into the dryer and stayed inside while it was operating, in which tossed her around and killed her in the process. Preston and the officer left the laundry room, returned outside to their cars.

They walked out of the front door as Preston turned to the officer.

"What was the relationship between the adult and teenager?"

"They were mother and daughter. It was just them in the house at the time. The mother divorced a few months back and took the daughter with her."

"Should we contact the father of the daughter regarding this incident?"

The officer turned and looked toward Preston and said, "I think its best we do that after we get the bodies out of the house."

Preston walked toward his car, but the officer called him back, he walked over to him. The officer looked at little nervous, as if he's about to ask a unusual question.

"Marshal, I have a question to ask you." The officer said

enthusiastically.

"Go for it, officer"

"Why do they call you "*The Instinct*" exactly? I never understood the reason for it."

Preston smiled, rubbing his chin and turning his head, looking in another direction. He exhaled slowly before turning and looked at the officer with a mild smile.

"Look at it this way, everyone has instincts in their own sense of perception. It's what makes us do what we do. I just tend to use it all the time. If not most of the time. No hesitation in place of my career. I don't second guess, unless it's confuses the living hell out of me."

"I've always been curious of why you're called that. It must be cool to have a nickname in this line of work."

"Not exactly. From my perspective, nicknames today are now overrated. Don't have any sense of meaning to them."

"Really?" said a voice from behind Preston.

Preston turned and saw his boss, Eldon Ross, the chief commissioner of the New Haven Marshal and Detective Agency. Eldon is a man in his early fifties, wearing a button-down shirt with a nice tie and slacks. Eldon looked at Preston with a glare as he turned to the officer.

"You really believe what Preston's telling you, officer? Because if you are, that just makes you nothing but a rookie in this field."

"Well, sir, he's the Instinct." The officer said without hesitation. "I meant to say, yes sir."

"The Instinct. The only thing Preston could possibly be is a hard-headed guy who doesn't listen to the instructions he's given. Instead, he makes up his own schedule of work and does what he wants whenever he wants. Try convincing me that he's using his gut to make those decisions."

"Eldon, what have I done this time for you to arrive here like this and call me out?"

"You know what you did. So, don't play those childlike games with me, Maddox. Your little incident from last night is quickly spreading around the entire agency and somewhat across the city. This isn't going to go well for you, me, or the agency."

"Eldon, let me explain the situation to you. A few weeks ago, I gave Cartel a choice to leave New Haven or he would meet us end by my hand. After those weeks had passed, I confronted him at one of his hiding spots, smuggling drugs. We talked for a bit as I gave him a short amount of time to leave and he made his decision right there. Besides, I've been on his trail for a few months now and it was getting tiresome."

Eldon shrugged his shoulders. "Yeah right. What else you have in terms of defense? Did you plan on talking him to death?"

"It was self-defense as well." Preston said. "He pulled first, and I fired the first shot. Which was the last shot before I called the police and coroner."

Eldon looked down and around the area as he rubbed his bald head. Glancing at the officers exiting the home. He looked at Preston. "Ok, once you're back at the office, we'll discuss all of this thoroughly and we'll find some way to get through your mess. alright."

"I'll see you back at the office, Eldon." Preston said as Eldon walked away from the area.

The officer walked over to Preston and said, "Jonny Cartel? The elite crime boss, Jonny Cartel."

"What about Cartel is getting you hyped up right now?"

"So, you really shot Jonny Cartel? You killed the bastard. How did it feel accomplishing it?"

Preston stared at the officer. He showed a faint smile before walking away.

"Something just had to be done about the man. That's all I can possibly say on the matter."

Preston walked to his car, gets inside and leaves the neighborhood, going to the Agency Office.

3

Preston arrived at the New Haven Marshal and Detective Agency. He walked into the front doors. Preston looked around and spotted everyone staring at him. Preston walked to the elevator and pressed the button. He stood waiting for the elevator door to open, so he can leave the lobby. One gentleman, wearing a grey suit walked by and looked at Preston. He does the same.

"Is there a problem, sir?" Preston said.

The gentleman turned his head and continued walking. Preston smiled as the elevator beeped and its door opened. He walked in and pressed the button for the third floor. The elevator door closed. He reached to the third floor and sees Eldon waiting for him in the head office. Preston walked toward the office as he passed by other detectives in their offices solving their own cases. Eldon sat behind his desk, surfing through the internet. He heard a knock on the door.

"Come on in, Preston."

Preston opened the door and walked in. "How did you know it was me that was walking through?"

"I can sense you from the elevator. Anyone can tell if you're in the building or not"

Preston smiled. "Funny. I'm sure you could. What did you need to talk to me about exactly?"

Eldon turned to Preston from the computer screen and looked at him with a gaze. Preston glanced his eyes a bit across the office.

"The reason why you're here Preston is because of the actions you took by killing Jonny Cartel. You know what you did was a big mistake?"

"Are you sure it was a mistake. Because from my point of view, the man had to be stopped one way or another."

"Well, this agency doesn't go by your point of view, it goes by its Chief's point of view. Meaning me."

"I got that well enough."

"So, because of your actions. With a lot of thought and right timing as well. I've decided that you need someone to watch what you're doing on these cases."

"Wait a minute. Just hold on a second. What exactly do you mean someone will be looking out for me? Are you implying a suggestion that I might have a partner?"

"Yes, Preston. That's exactly what I'm suggesting. Look, this is how I see it. You shot Jonny Cartel out in the open with no hesitation. So, if you were to come across someone with a similar history, you would do the same to them. If not worse."

"Of course, that's the way I do my job. Besides, Eldon, I already told you that it was self-defense. Cartel pulled out his weapon first, he also threatened to kill me. So, what else was I supposed to do."

"You could've called backup you know."

"Call backup?" Preston said. "It wasn't that big of a deal. We were the only two there after he commanded his guys to leave."

Eldon leaned back in his chair, rocking in it to relax himself and feel comfortable. "So, overall, what's the big problem about having a partner?"

"My last partner worked on both sides of the law and to make it even crazier, the guy was a snitch."

"A snitch you say. Good thing your new partner only works on one side of the law. Our side of the law and I'll also add that she's very good at what she does anyway."

"Wait. She?" Preston said with a raised voice.

"Well, of course, Preston. Your new partner is a she. There's not a problem is there?"

Eldon looked at the door and waved his hand, signaled someone to come in. The individual walked in and stood by the door, just a few inches from where Preston sat. He hasn't looked behind him yet to see his new partner.

"Preston, here's your new partner. In the flesh I should say."

"Preston smirked. "Really. Let me get a good look at her."

Preston turned and sees his new partner. He looked at her from head to toe. She had nice straight blonde hair that reached near her shoulders and she wore a pair of blue jeans with a white buttoned-down shirt and a brown leather jacket to go with it. Preston smiled at her. She showed no emotion toward him, but only gave him a significant stare. As if she had no trust in him of any measure. Preston turned back to Eldon, smirking.

"This beautiful young woman is Emily Weston. A fellow United States Marshal and Detective from Newark in the state of New Jersey."

Preston turned again. "It's a pleasure to meet you, Ms. Weston."

"Same here." Emily said. "You look different than what I've heard."

"Do tell what you've heard about me. I'm sure the tales were pleasant enough to share to everyone, meaning me, myself, and I."

"Just that your what they call an angry man whose hell bent on claiming justice and changing the ways of civilization as we know it. Using your gun as the holy grail."

Preston laughed as Eldon chucked a bit. Emily stayed quiet with only a face with no emotion of any kind. Preston stopped laughing and noticed Emily's face. Eldon gave one more chuckle before glancing at Emily.

Emily is in her late twenties and her confidence gave her the shine of a woman who stood independent, able to get the job done. She looked toward Eldon.

"I've heard quite enough information about the murders that occurred in the neighborhood last night. I was only wondering how the investigation is currently operating?"

"The investigation is currently ongoing." said Eldon. "But, since you asked about it, you and Preston can go to the neighborhood and asks some of the neighbors about anything unusual that occurred that night."

"That's interesting enough to hear."

Preston looked at them both with a grin. Thinking to himself if he should give some words toward them. As the words near his tongue, he decides otherwise not to speak them.

"Um, pardon me, Eldon, I was planning on going over to a location where I know some answers could be currently available."

"That's Great. Even a better idea I could add to that. Since you brought it up and you apparently want some company, why don't you go ahead and take Emily with you on this."

"She can't go with me on this one." Preston said while smiling. "Besides, she's a well-established novice here in New Haven and no offense to her, but, I don't play well with others when it comes to the law and my tasks."

Emily turned to Preston and stared him in the eyes like a predator inching for a bite toward its prey.

"I could say the same about myself. In Newark, I did most

of my work alone and had some help in some cases. So, look Preston, unlike some of the women that you've come across and met in your days, I'm not one of them. Nor do I fit in their caliber in any way, shape, or form. I'm just a woman that gets the job done whenever I can, however I can. With or without your assistance."

"Really?" Preston said. "You're saying you're some type of new breed of female detective. I'm sure I could dig up something from your past back in Jersey that could shake you up a bit."

"Not exactly. You'll hardly find anything on me that could lead to your gloating habits."

Emily turned to Eldon and asked for the address to the murder location. Eldon gave her the file of the location. She walked out of the office. Preston stood up and watched as Emily walked to the elevator. She turned to Eldon. Eldon is smirking at Preston.

"Listen, just try to work with her Preston." Eldon said. "Just try, please."

"Sure thing, I'll try. But, I won't like it." Preston said.

Preston left the office as Eldon goes back to the computer, still smiling about Preston's attitude toward Emily. Preston is outside as Emily waited for him at his car. Preston slowly walked towards the car. He sees Emily standing by the passenger's seat. He pointed at her and the car.

"Mind if I ask where's your car?"

"I thought I'll ride with you if you don't mind me." Emily said. "Don't want to waste gas on mine. You should be alright with that I presume."

Preston looked with a glint and said, "You have a nice valid point there."

Preston took out the keys and unlocked the car. Emily sits on the passenger's side as Preston sits into the driver's seat. He started the car and they left the office, driving to the neighborhood.

"Though, I hope you're standing next to the car when I unlock it. So, that way I won't drive off without you and you can call on a cab to pick you up and drop you off."

As they drove down the streets, Emily turned and stared outside her window at all the locations around the area that they've passed by. Preston noticed and slightly turned toward her direction and watched her as she glanced the surrounding locations. Many vehicles are passing by as Preston entered onto the freeway. The number of passing and surrounding vehicles gives Emily a questioning though.

"Looking for something out there?" Preston asked. "You seem very on point looking at these places is all."

"No. I just never knew that New Haven was this crowded." Emily said. "Though it would be much smaller than what I'm currently seeing."

"We have our moments. Some days are good while the rest are bad. We get through it all. So, what brought you here to begin with?"

"Things became quiet around Newark, so I began looking for another location to work. Later, the agency began recruiting and some of the new detectives went to Newark and I was moved here."

"By the look on your face and the tone in your voice, you don't sound to happy about your transfer. Are you happy?"

"Honestly, I didn't expect to come here." Emily said. "I'm one of the best US Marshals in this country, so I believed they would send me to bigger places like New York, L.A., Miami, Las Vegas, Houston. Just somewhere big."

Preston smiled.

"Very soon, Ms. Weston, you'll realize that New Haven is

bigger than it looks to be."

Emily looked. "Can't wait for that."

Currently at the New Haven Airport is Billy Bronson, a scruffy, scrawny, slim man who's wearing a flannel shirt with jeans and a denim jacket, also wearing a baseball cap. He walked towards the tunnel, seeing a lot of passengers walking in and out. He stood at the tunnel, scouted the area looking for someone. He caught someone from a distance and started straining his eyes to get a better look.

"Please let that be him." Billy said.

He finally sees the individual he's come to pick up. Billy walked over to him.

"There's my guy!"

The individual is known as Hoyt Bennett, a man in his late thirties, whose slim with bold features and hair that looked as if it's never been washed or combed. He's also wearing a long-sleeved buttoned shirt with jeans and black dress shoes. Hoyt walked over to Billy, smiling.

"Well, isn't it the great Billy Bronson. We meet once again in this crazy nonstop lifetime of ours."

"Hoyt Bennett. How long has it been, pal?"

They shook hands as Hoyt hugged Billy and patted him on the back. Billy decided to do the same. Hoyt picked up his bags as they walked through the airport.

"How have things been in New Haven since my little departure?"

"You know how this place works. The same old situation with the same old people. Sometimes, even new folks that comes across these ways."

"Billy, I'll say this. It's time to get things going since I'm back in town."

"How so? What do you have planned already?"

"In short words, Billy, it's time to blow some shit up."

Hoyt continued to smile as he started walking toward the exit doors of the airport Billy slowly followed him outside. Shaking his head in uncertainly as to what's being planned in Hoyt's head.

"Take the damn shot."

"Yes sir."

Cody stood still and fired the shot. The round went through the hole of the window and flew through the air, inching near the hit man, who continued firing at the upstairs floor. Eldon and Darius were stilled ducked underneath the windows. The round went pass the brick wall and hit the hit man in the chest. Holding his chest, the hit man crouched down as he fell to the ground. Not hearing anymore gun fire, Eldon and Darius took a small look out the window and saw the hit man down on the ground, slowly moving.

"So, we're going to the roof to check if he's still breathing?" Darius said.

"Something like that." Eldon said. "Let's get up there."

Upon reaching the other building and making it to the rooftop, other police officers with many officials had arrived at the scene as well. They make the discovery that the hit man survived the sniper shot from Cody as the officer slowly placed the hit man in the back of the police car. Shutting the back door, they thanked Eldon and his marshals for helping out with the cause and drive off. Eldon turned and told Cody that he was good at keeping his eyes open at his surroundings, otherwise, they probably wouldn't have caught the hit man. Eldon walked over to another officer.

"Did you find the name of the hit man, officer?" Eldon said. "Because, we didn't have any sort of information on the fellow."

"We don't have any knowledge of his real name, sir." The officer said. "From what we've gathered, the name he goes by is The Jackal. Something within that category."

"What's all on his record?" Eldon said.

"According to his criminal records, The Jackal was one of the country's most primary hit men. He primarily completed jobs and tasks for certain companies who were involved with the prostitution business. He also did some small duty in the marijuana business and the crystal meth business."

"So, he was basically killing off prostitutes because he was paid by a competitor to do so." Eldon said. "Never knew a job like that ever existed."

"Though, we hope to question him as soon as he recovers. We should have more information tomorrow at noon, hopefully. We'll contact you when we've gathered enough information."

"Thank you, officer." Eldon said.

Eldon walked over to Darius and Cody, who were discussing the type of rifle The Jackal used for his assassinations. They turned toward Eldon as he approached them in a slow manner.

"What's next on the agenda now, chief?" Darius said. "Any more places we should probably be looking out for."

"I'm going to get a drink." Eldon said. "I would assume that the two of you would be coming along with me? Just to celebrate what we've just accomplished here."

"Sure." Cody said. "I'm up for it."

AVAILABLE NOW WHEREVER BOOKS ARE SOLD AND FROM DARK TITAN DIRECT

ABOUT THE AUTHOR

Ty'Ron W. C. Robinson II is the author of several works of fiction. Including the *Dark Titan Universe Saga*, *The Haunted City Saga*, *EverWar Universe*, *Symbolum Venatores*, *Frightened!*, *Instincts*, *Chevah Mythos*, *The Horde*, *Argoron*, *The Supreme Pursuer*, *Vanok*, *Dark Titan's The Dead Days*, and *Agent Trevor*.

Also of other books (*The Book of The Elect, etc.*) and One-Shot short stories.

More information pertaining to the author and stories can be found at darktitanentertainment.com.

Twitter: @TyRonRobinsonII
Vero: @tyronrobinsonii

Twitter: @DarkTitan_
Instagram: @darktitanentertainment
Facebook: @DarkTitanEnt

www.ingramcontent.com/pod-product-compliance
Lightning Source LLC
LaVergne TN
LVHW041545070526
838199LV00046B/1833